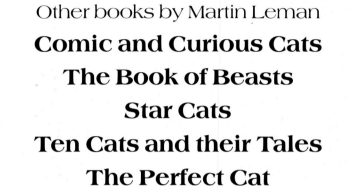

Other books by Martin Leman

Comic and Curious Cats

The Book of Beasts

Star Cats

Ten Cats and their Tales

The Perfect Cat

First published in Great Britain in 1982 by
Pelham Books Ltd, 44 Bedford Square, London WC1B 3DU
Reprinted 1983, 1984

Copyright © Jill and Martin Leman 1982

ISBN 0 7207 14036

Printed and bound in Italy by
New Interlitho, Milan

TWELVE
CATS
FOR CHRISTMAS

MARTIN LEMAN

PELHAM BOOKS

On the first day of Christmas
my true love gave to me
**a black cat
in a pear tree**

On the second day of Christmas
my true love gave to me

a stripy ginger
kitten

and a black cat in a pear tree

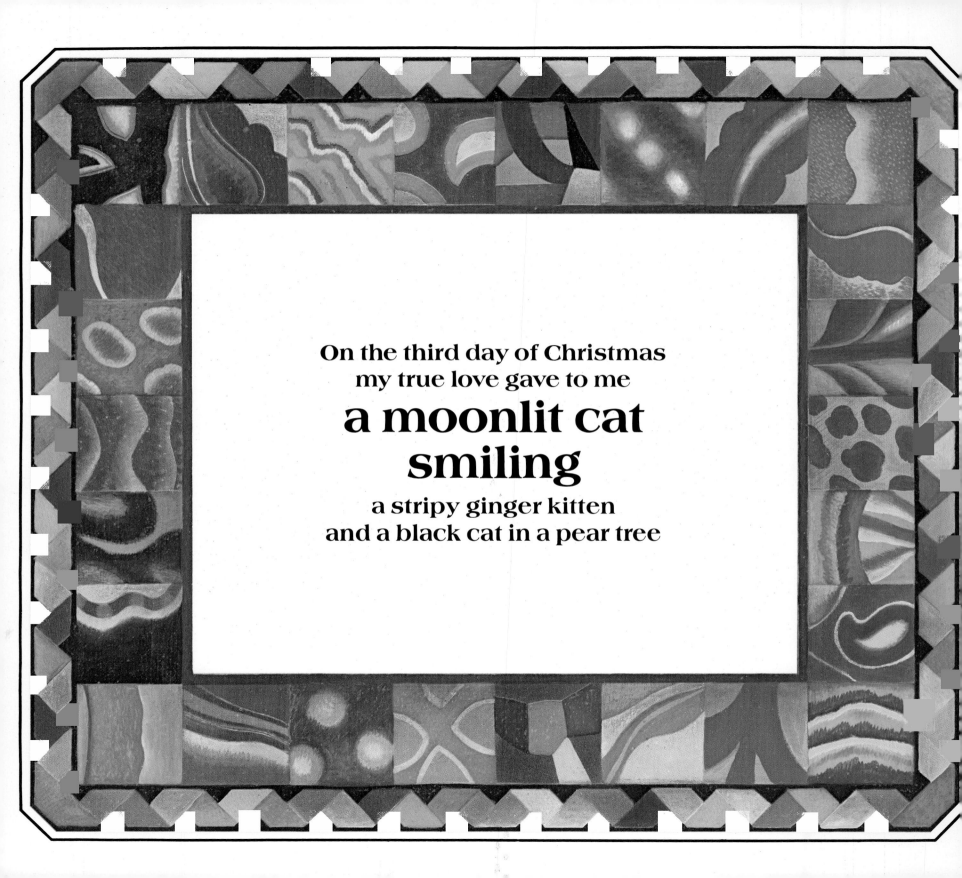

On the third day of Christmas
my true love gave to me

a moonlit cat
smiling

a stripy ginger kitten
and a black cat in a pear tree

On the fourth day of Christmas
my true love gave to me

an amber cat resting

a moonlit cat smiling
a stripy ginger kitten
and a black cat in a pear tree

On the fifth day of Christmas
my true love gave to me
a fat little
tabby

an amber cat resting
a moonlit cat smiling
a stripy ginger kitten
and a black cat in a pear tree

On the sixth day of Christmas
my true love gave to me

a white cat
waiting

a fat little tabby
an amber cat resting
a moonlit cat smiling
a stripy ginger kitten
and a black cat in a pear tree

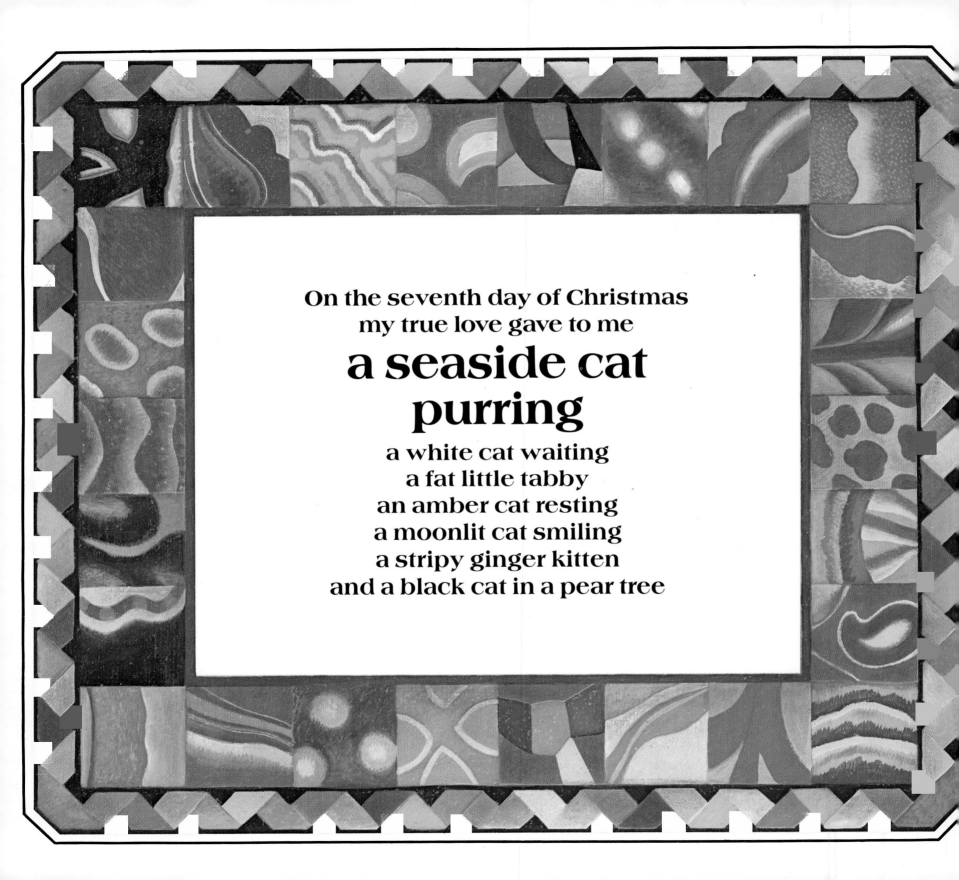

On the seventh day of Christmas
my true love gave to me

a seaside cat
purring

a white cat waiting
a fat little tabby
an amber cat resting
a moonlit cat smiling
a stripy ginger kitten
and a black cat in a pear tree

On the eighth day of Christmas
my true love gave to me

a small cat hiding

a seaside cat purring
a white cat waiting
a fat little tabby
an amber cat resting
a moonlit cat smiling
a stripy ginger kitten
and a black cat in a pear tree

On the ninth day of Christmas
my true love gave to me

a naughty cat playing

a small cat hiding
a seaside cat purring
a white cat waiting
a fat little tabby
an amber cat resting
a moonlit cat smiling
a stripy ginger kitten
and a black cat in a pear tree

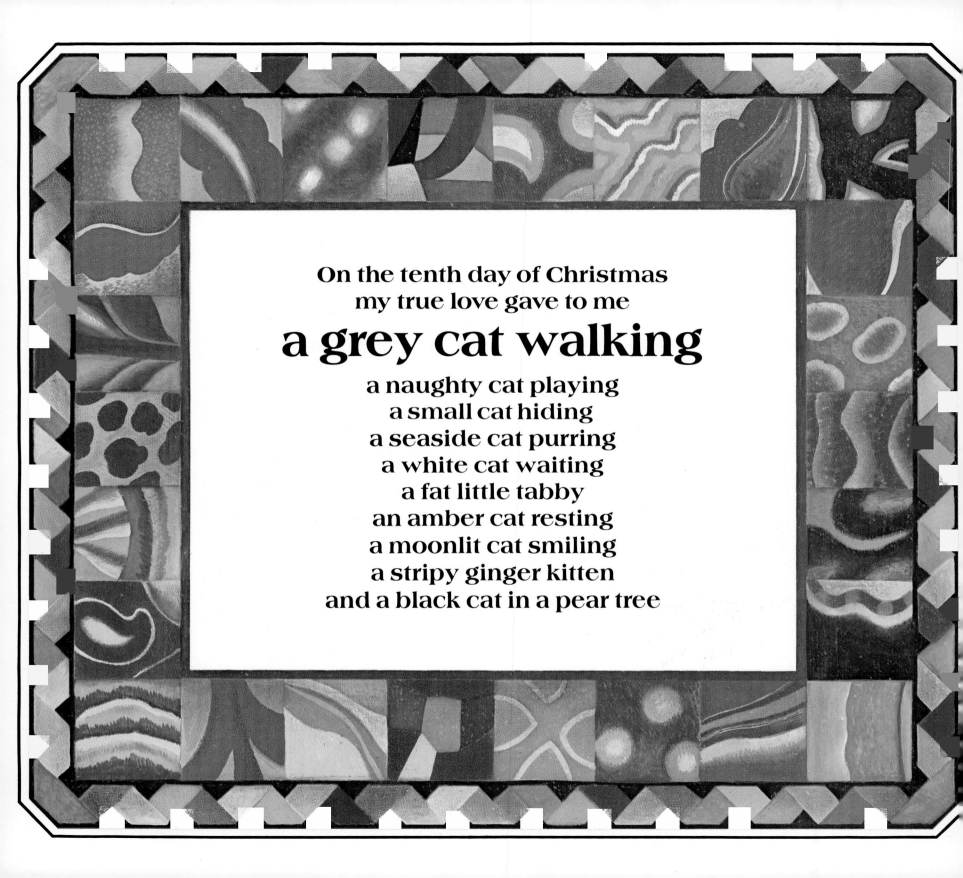

On the tenth day of Christmas
my true love gave to me

a grey cat walking

a naughty cat playing
a small cat hiding
a seaside cat purring
a white cat waiting
a fat little tabby
an amber cat resting
a moonlit cat smiling
a stripy ginger kitten
and a black cat in a pear tree

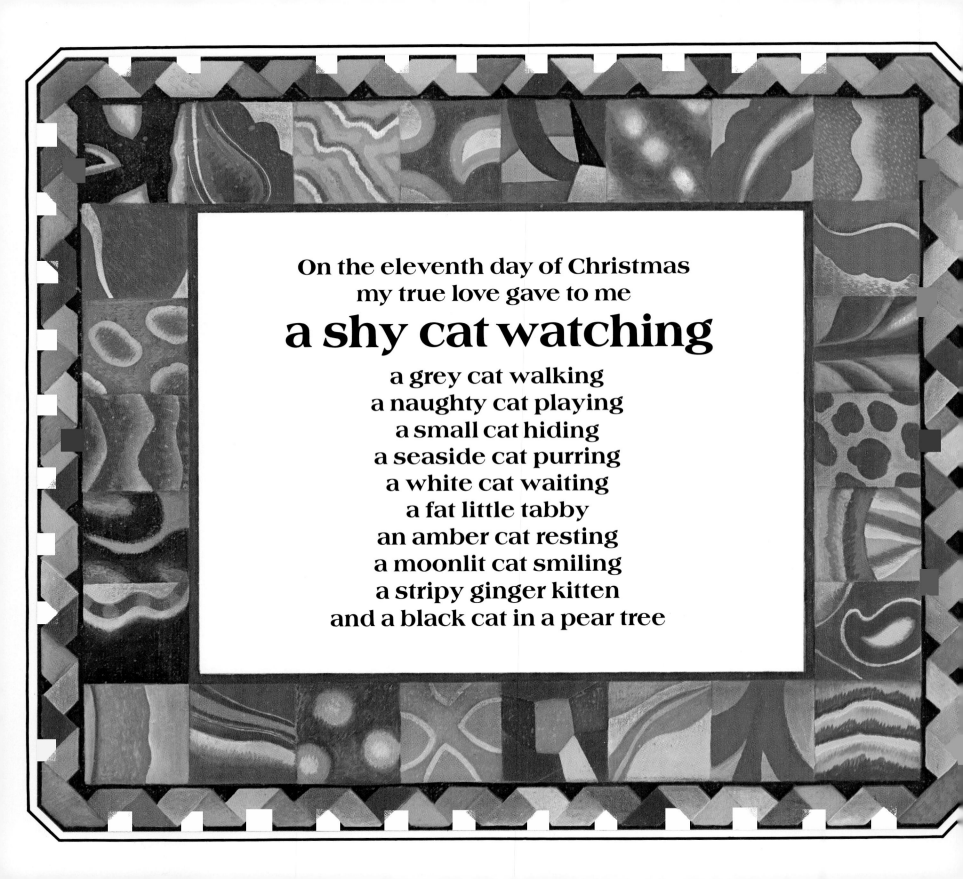

On the eleventh day of Christmas
my true love gave to me

a shy cat watching

a grey cat walking
a naughty cat playing
a small cat hiding
a seaside cat purring
a white cat waiting
a fat little tabby
an amber cat resting
a moonlit cat smiling
a stripy ginger kitten
and a black cat in a pear tree

On the twelfth day of Christmas
my true love gave to me

a dozy cat napping

a shy cat watching
a grey cat walking
a naughty cat playing
a small cat hiding
a seaside cat purring
a white cat waiting
a fat little tabby
an amber cat resting
a moonlit cat smiling
a stripy ginger kitten
and a black cat in a pear tree